Father's Chinese Opera

Father's Chinese Opera

Rich Lo

Sky Pony Press
New York

Father was the band leader and composer of the Chinese opera in Hong Kong.

Sometimes I sat on
top of the instrument
cases and watched
the actors onstage.

They sang high-pitched songs
Father had written. They did
flips and somersaults.

And pretended to fight
all across the stage.

One evening after rehearsal, I walked backstage to talk with Gai Chui. Everyone said Gai Chui was the best acrobat in the Chinese opera. He taught the troupe to perform acrobatic moves choreographed to Father's music.

"Will you teach me the acrobatic moves?" I asked.

"I will be your
best student!"

"I will practice
day and night!"

"I will master
all the moves!"

Finally, Gai Chui agreed. He and
I started to exercise together.

As we practiced the moves, he called out the names and the movements of the animals we were imitating.

Praying Mantis!

Drunken Monkey!

Crouching Tiger!

Striking Leopard!

Flying Dragon!

White Crane!

I boasted to all my friends
that I would soon be joining
the opera as an acrobat.

But when I went backstage after one performance to tell Gai Chui that I was ready for my assignment, he laughed loudly.

"Presumptuous boy! Do you think you can be part of the opera so quickly?"

I ran from the tent all the way back to our apartment. I sat by the window and stared at the people on the street below.

I felt Father touch my shoulder.

He showed me a photograph of him holding an old ewu case. "That photograph was taken before my first audition in Quanzhou," he said. "I had to learn to play all the instruments so I could write the music. And I had to learn to write songs before I had the chance to lead an opera troupe."

As I lay in bed that night, I thought about what Father had said. The next day I returned to the tent where the actors and acrobats were practicing.

At the other end of the stage, I could see the young flag carriers practicing their routines.

I asked Father for permission to be a flag carrier. He smiled and said, "Yes, but just for the summer." I began to practice with the flag carriers. The group's leader handed out flags and we ran in single file, weaving like a serpent on the front of the stage.

I made many new friends, including some of the younger acrobats. They told me that they were once flag carriers and had continued to practice until they were good enough to work with the regular acrobats.

I practiced even
harder with the
other flag carriers.

After the last performance of the summer, I saw
Gai Chui standing on the side of the stage.

"Did you see the moves I made?" I asked.

Chui looked at the stage, then at me. "You are very good," he said. "Keep practicing and you will become the best acrobat in the opera."

Author's Note
Chinese Opera

Chinese opera is a form of dramatic musical theater, first organized during the Tang Dynasty under Emperor Xuanzong in the years 712–755. Opera themes are usually about family goodness, poverty and wealth, shame, revolution, and war. Every story is written to educate the audience about life. Actors use exaggerated movements and sing songs in different pitches to entertain the audience.

Actors wear colorful makeup and traditional costumes, with each color having a different meaning: white is evil; red is bravery; blue is loyalty; yellow is ambition; and black is fierceness. The costumes are unique to the actors based on the characters they play. The more important the character, the more decorations on the costume. For example, a war general will have a highly decorated outfit with feathers, small flags, and his name on the back. A peasant will just have a plain outfit with a sash.

Chinese opera also consists of acrobats who bring action to the play with their martial arts feats, somersaults, and flips. The acrobats are young men and women who have aspirations to become actors. Through martial arts training, they gain balance and strength to enhance their acting and singing on stage during a long performance.

Beneath the acrobats are the flag carriers. They, too, must learn martial arts in the hope that they will be promoted to acrobats. They usually carry lightweight flags made of silk embroidered with Chinese characters. They add excitement and action in the background during fight scenes. For example, a flag carrier with the name of the emperor on his flag will lead an army of acrobats running in single file like a serpent on stage.

The songs are the core of the opera. They are written by composers who have deep knowledge of literature, history, and music. The opera music is influenced by songs and stories of ancient times. The lyrics are changed to fit the scenes, but the melody is seldom altered. Throughout the play, the audience recognizes these familiar melodies.

Lo Tok

Like other composers, my father Lo Tok was also an orchestra leader for the Chinese opera. Born in 1926, he started playing Chinese instruments at nine years old and was performing in public by eleven. He was raised by his mother because his father immigrated to Panama to avoid persecution by the Chinese Nationalists and the Japanese invaders.

My father went to college to study science, but music was his main interest. In addition to other instruments, he taught himself to play the violin and erhu. He and my mother were married in 1944. By 1946, with the birth of #1 Sister (parents often used numbers to identify which sibling was older) he began to play music in small theaters and on the street. In collaboration with singers, he made just enough money to support his small family, and two years later, he was playing regularly in theaters with daily pay.

In 1957, I was born, and our family now consisted of three girls and two boys. Father was growing weary of life under the Communist party even though he was not persecuted because he was able to read and play music. People who could read—and who were entertainers—were considered an asset to the community.

That same year, my grandmother decided to immigrate to Panama to join my grandfather. Mother, along with my older brother and me, accompanied Grandmother to Hong Kong to send her off on an ocean liner. Mother decided to stay in Hong Kong and help arrange for my father and three sisters to escape from China. Father was not able to travel outside of China because he was considered a valued person. So, he and my three sisters bribed their way to get on a ship to Macau, a small island off the coast of China. From there, they sailed in a small boat to Hong Kong, undetected, at night. Because Mother and Father had been communicating through mail, Mother knew approximately when they would be arriving. Father had the address of the apartment where we stayed and soon my entire family was reunited.

In Hong Kong, Father found work easily because he had developed a reputation as a composer and great musician. He was offered a night slot at a popular radio station. He quickly assembled a band and began his rise as a band leader. He was noticed by opera troupes and received offers to compose songs and lead orchestras. He shortly became a household name.

Since I wasn't old enough to be in school, Father took me to the theater for the opera rehearsals and performances. People clapped whenever he met a crowd at the theaters. They treated us like royalty.

Father composed at night, usually in a dimly lit room. I often slept alongside him and would awaken to the sound of him humming a melody as he wrote lyrics. Father would then take me to a dim sum restaurant for breakfast. It was a happy time for our family.

By 1962, Father was a star in the Chinese opera. Famous actors and musicians came to our apartment regularly—eating, drinking, talking, and singing. I met many theater people, including the head of the acrobats, Gai Chui. Father told me that Gai Chui was the best teacher and choreographer of martial art moves in the opera. I saw him practice with the other acrobats backstage at the theater and wished very much to be like him, but I was too young.

In 1964, Grandfather arranged for the family to immigrate to the United States. We arrived in Los Angeles, California, and settled in a house on a corner lot outside Chinatown—at the foothill of Dodger Stadium. Language was immediately a problem for Father. He was proud of his Chinese culture and wasn't able to put that aside to learn English. He also became a victim of bad advice, false promises, and the pressure of having to support a large family. He could have taught in a university, but this was the early 1960s and racism, ignorance, and wars with Asian countries had made many Americans prejudiced against those they considered "non-Americans."

Although my father continued to play instruments, coming to America was the end of his career as a musician and composer. During the next twenty-five years, he worked as a cook and a failed owner of a Chinese restaurant.

Today, at eighty-nine, he lives with my mother in an apartment building for seniors. He no longer plays his instruments with skill because of a series of strokes, but he still writes, paints, and loves to talk about his fame—a short but very positive time of his life.

As an adult, I understand the events that shaped my father's life. He gave up a career as a famous composer to keep his family together in a country with a new language and culture. He went from being a renowned writer of poetry and music to being illiterate in America.

My siblings and I benefited greatly from the strength of both our parents. They gave us the opportunity to be productive professionals—to raise our families with high standards. I believe the torch has passed to me, that I carry the responsibility of being a contributor to the arts and of showing that it is possible to live my dreams while sharing the Chinese experience.

—Rich Lo

Further Reading

Chinese Opera
Jessica Tan Gudnason, Gong Li, Li Gong
Abbeville Press

Chinese Opera: Images and Stories
Siu Wang-Ngai, Peter Lovrick, Wang-Ngai Siu
University of Washington Press

Chinese Opera Costumes Paper Dolls
Ming-Ju Sun
Dover Publications

Lady White Snake: A Tale From Chinese Opera
Aaron Shepard (Author), Song Nan Zhang (Illustrator)
Pan Asian Publications

Peking Opera (Introductions to Chinese Culture)
Chengbei Xu
Cambridge University Press

Sky Pony Press books may be purchased in bulk at special discounts for sales promotion, corporate gifts, fund-raising, or educational purposes. Special editions can also be created to specifications. For details, contact the Special Sales Department, Sky Pony Press, 307 West 36th Street, 11th Floor, New York, NY 10018 or info@skyhorsepublishing.com.

Sky Pony® is a registered trademark of Skyhorse Publishing, Inc.®, a Delaware corporation.

Visit our website at www.skyponypress.com.

10 9 8 7 6 5 4 3 2 1

Manufactured in China, February 2014
This product conforms to CPSIA 2008

Library of Congress Cataloging-in-Publication Data

Lo, Rich, author, illustrator.
 Father's Chinese opera / Rich Lo.
      pages cm
 Summary: "A little boy wishes to join his father's
Chinese opera but learns that you must work hard
in order to reach your goals. With an author's note
at the end"-- Provided by publisher.
 ISBN 978-1-62873-610-6 (hardback)
 [1. Opera, Chinese--Fiction. 2. Perseverance
(Ethics)--Fiction. 3. Acrobatics--Fiction. 4.
Fathers and sons--Fiction. 5. China--Fiction.] I.
Title.
 PZ7.L778788Fat 2014
 [E]--dc23

2013041609